William Shakespeare's
A Midsummer Night's Dream

Tamara Hollingsworth
and Harriet Isecke, M.S.Ed.

Publishing Credits

Dona Herweck Rice, *Editor-in-Chief*; Lee Aucoin, *Creative Director*; Don Tran, *Print Production Manager;* Timothy J. Bradley, *Illustration Manager*; Wendy Conklin, M.A., *Senior Editor*; Torrey Maloof, *Associate Editor*; Lesley Palmer, *Cover Designer;* Rusty Kinnunen, *Illustrator;* Stephanie Reid, *Photo Editor*; Rachelle Cracchiolo, M.A. Ed., *Publisher*

Image Credits

cover & p.1 German print illustrating a scene from Shakespeare's *A Midsummer Night's Dream*, showing Oberon and Titania, the fairy king and queen. Hulton Archive/Getty Images

Teacher Created Materials

5301 Oceanus Drive
Huntington Beach, CA 92649-1030
http://www.tcmpub.com
ISBN 978-1-4333-1275-5
©2010 Teacher Created Materials, Inc.
Reprinted 2013

A Midsummer Night's Dream

Story Summary

In *A Midsummer Night's Dream*, the fairy king, Oberon, is angry with his wife, Titania. He enlists the help of a mischievous sprite named Puck to get back at her. Oberon's plan goes awry when Puck makes some foolish mistakes with the enchantments. Four humans find themselves mixed up in the strange and confusing events that night in the woods.

Tips for Performing Reader's Theater

Adapted from Aaron Shepard

- Do not let your script hide your face. If you cannot see the audience, your script is too high.

- Look up often when you speak. Do not just look at your script.

- Speak slowly so the audience knows what you are saying.

- Speak loudly so everyone can hear you.

- Speak with feeling. If the character is sad, let your voice be sad. If the character is surprised, let your voice be surprised.

- Stand up straight. Keep your hands and feet still.

- Remember that even when you are not speaking, you are still your character.

Tips for Performing
Reader's Theater *(cont.)*

- If the audience laughs, wait for the laughter to stop before you speak again.

- If someone in the audience talks, do not pay attention.

- If someone walks into the room, do not pay attention.

- If you make a mistake, pretend it was right.

- If you drop something, try to leave it where it is until the audience is looking somewhere else.

- If a reader forgets to read his or her part, see if you can read the part instead, make something up, or just skip over it. Do not whisper to the reader!

A Midsummer Night's Dream

Characters

Hermia	Lysander
Helena	Puck
Oberon	Demetrius

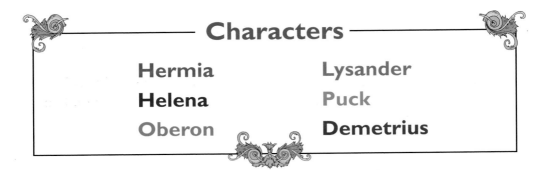

Setting

This reader's theater is set in Athens and the woods that surround the city's walls. It begins outside the palace of Theseus, the Duke of Athens. The remainder of the play occurs in the woods.

Act I, Scene I

Outside the palace of Theseus

Hermia: Lysander, my heart is crushed! Father has ordered me to marry Demetrius and not you, my love. He even has Theseus involved.

Lysander: And what did Theseus say?

Hermia: He called me headstrong. He told me that if I disobey my father and refuse to marry Demetrius, I will be punished.

Lysander: Punished? How?

Hermia: I could be sent away to a convent to live as a nun for the rest of my life! Or, I may even be executed! Theseus gave me only until the day he weds Hippolyta to acquiesce to my father's demands. That is four days away!

Lysander: How did you reply, my love?

Hermia: I told Theseus that I would rather have whatever punishment he gave me than a life without you, Lysander.

Lysander:	Ay, me! The course of true love never did run smooth. I do not understand why your father wants you to marry Demetrius and not me. You have freely pledged your love to me, Hermia. Is it not love that is more important than all?
Hermia:	Oh, but it is, my sweet Lysander!
Lysander:	I do not think Demetrius is faithful. Not long ago, he was engaged to your friend, Helena. She is still in love with him and follows him everywhere.
Hermia:	I find this all too terrible to think about.
Lysander:	I have an idea! My dear aunt, who thinks of me as her own son, lives on the other side of the woods. We can leave and go there. Then I may marry you!
Hermia:	But what about Theseus?
Lysander:	It is far enough away so Theseus's decision and the harsh laws of Athens cannot affect us. If you love me, you will sneak out of your father's house tomorrow night and meet me in the woods.

Hermia: I swear to you, by Cupid's strongest bow and best arrow, that I will be there. Look, here comes Helena.

Lysander: Hello, Helena. How are you today?

Helena: I am truly miserable. All Demetrius ever talks about is you, Hermia. He tells me how your eyes are like stars and your voice is as sweet as a lark's. Oh, Hermia, teach me how to be like you so that he will love me.

Hermia: I promise you that I do not encourage him. I frown upon him, yet he still loves me.

Helena: I wish I could encourage him to love me again. Before he met you, all he did was compliment and flatter me. Then you came, and all those beautiful words disappeared.

Hermia: I do not understand. The more I hate him, the more he loves me.

Helena: The more I love him, the more he hates me.

Hermia:	Well, take comfort, my friend, for he shall see my face no more. Lysander and I have made plans to run away and get married. We are going to meet in the woods tomorrow night.
Helena:	Oh, how exciting! I wish I knew how to inspire Demetrius to love me. Look, I see him now. I think I will try to speak with him. Good luck, Hermia and Lysander! I bid you farewell.
Hermia:	Goodbye, friend.
Lysander:	Goodbye, Helena.
Helena:	Demetrius, wait! I have something to tell you.
Demetrius:	Oh, Helena. Go away!
Helena:	But it is about Hermia.
Demetrius:	What about the beautiful Hermia?
Helena:	She and Lysander plan to meet in the woods and run away together.
Demetrius:	No! I must stop them.

Act II, Scene I

The woods outside of Athens

Puck: King Oberon, I came as quickly as I could and graciously I bow down before you as your merry sprite and servant. But you look glum today, King. Why are you so downtrodden?

Oberon: I am furious at my wife, Titania. All I want is that little human boy she keeps. I want him to be my henchman, but Titania will not let me have him.

Puck: Why would she refuse you this young boy?

Oberon: She says that his mother was a loving friend of hers. His mother was a mere mortal and died during childbirth. Titania claims that for the sake of that mother, she is raising the child. I will make her pay for this insult.

Puck: What will you do, King Oberon?

Oberon: Puck, do you remember the night when I heard a mermaid sing such an enchanting song that it calmed the stormy seas?

Puck: Yes, I remember it quite clearly.

Oberon: That same night, I saw Cupid flying from the cold moon to Earth. He shot his arrow at the most beautiful girl with enough love to pierce one hundred thousand hearts. But, his arrow missed.

Puck: What happened to the arrow, King Oberon?

Oberon: It landed on that island in a field of flowers, and its love dust powdered the field. I need you to fetch some flowers from that field.

Puck: What good are these flowers?

Oberon: When put on sleeping eyelids, the pollen of these flowers will make the sleeper fall in love with the next living thing it sees upon waking. Please go and fetch some for me as quickly as possible.

Puck: Of course! I will swiftly procure these flowers for you and return in a flash.

Oberon: When you do return, I will have you place the pollen from the flowers on Titania's eyelids so that the next thing she sees—be it lion, bear, wolf, or bull—she will fall madly in love with, and I will get that boy. I hear people coming. Go, Puck! I will make myself invisible and listen to what these mortals have to say.

Act II, Scene II

The woods

Helena: Wait, Demetrius! Did you hear the craftsmen in the woods getting ready for the play? It will be for the wedding of Theseus and Hippolyta. The title is "The Most Sorrowful Comedy and Awful Death of Pyramus and Thisbe."

Demetrius: I am not interested in the play or what you have to say about it, Helena.

Helena: But the parts seem so funny. Bottom is playing Pyramus, a young man who kills himself for love. Flute is playing Thisbe, the lover of Pyramus. Did you see how terribly upset Flute became when he was told he had a girl's part and had to make his voice sound more feminine?

Demetrius: I do not care! Stop talking, Helena, and stop following me! Did I ask you to follow me? Did I say lovely words to encourage you? No! I have told you again and again that I do not love you.

Helena: But I love you so much that I must follow you.

Demetrius: You told me that Hermia and Lysander were running away into these woods. Where are they?

Helena: Do not worry, Demetrius, we will find them.

Demetrius: Not we, just I. What can I say to make you go away, Helena?

Helena: Nothing! Whatever harsh words you say, I just love you all the more.

Demetrius: It makes me sick to look at you.

Helena: It makes me sick not to look at you.

Demetrius: I will simply run away from you then.

Helena: *(shouting)* Run all you want, Demetrius. I will follow you and make a heaven out of hell!

Oberon: Do not worry, beautiful girl. I know I am invisible to you and you cannot hear me, but I have seen everything. Before you leave these woods, your young man will dote on you with the same loving devotion you have given to him. Ah, Puck, I see you have returned. Did you gather the flowers?

Puck: Yes, King Oberon, here are the flowers harboring the magic pollen.

Oberon:	Good. Now, listen carefully. Go dust Titania's eyes with this pollen. Be sure the timing is right. When she awakes, I want her to fall in love with someone who will cause her great humiliation. I have one more favor to ask of you, Puck.
Puck:	Whatever you desire, King Oberon.
Oberon:	Also take some of these flowers and travel through the woods. There is a young woman who is madly in love with a young man who scorns her. Dust some of the pollen upon his eyelids so that he will fall in love with her.
Puck:	I will do as you wish, my good king.

Poem: Sonnet 57

Act II, Scene III

In another part of the woods

Lysander:	Hermia, you are tired and I am not sure where we are. Let us make camp here for the night.
Hermia:	That is fine, Lysander. I will make my bed over there.

Lysander:	Then I will make my bed there, as well.
Hermia:	Not so fast, my dear Lysander. Lie over there, please.
Lysander:	But, Hermia, you have my heart and with it comes all of me. I have given an oath of my love, so why should we not lie close together?
Hermia:	Those are pretty words, Lysander, but lie over there, please.
Lysander:	If that is what you wish, I will do it. Good night my love, sweet dreams.
Hermia:	Good night, sweet friend. My love for you will not alter as long as I live.
Puck:	Aw, this must be the young man and woman about whom Oberon was speaking, for look how far apart they are from each other. If they were in love, they would be lying closer together. I will place the pollen upon your eyelids, young man, and when you waken, your love for her will surely grow, but only awaken after I go.

Helena: Oh, I cannot keep up with Demetrius. Who is this on the ground? Lysander! Are you dead or asleep? I see no blood, no wound. Lysander, if you live, good sir, awake! Awake, please!

Lysander: Oh radiant and glorious, Helena! Where is that foul Demetrius? I will meet him with my sword.

Helena: Lysander, what are you talking about? You love Hermia, and she loves you.

Lysander: Hermia? No, no, not Hermia. I love you, Helena. Who would not change a raven for a dove? The will of a man is swayed by reason, and my reason says that you are the worthier woman.

Helena: Why are you making fun of me, Lysander? What have I ever done to you to deserve this scorn? I thought you were a better man than that. I am leaving this instant!

Lysander: Do not leave, Helena, for I love you more than words can say. Wherever you go, I shall go, too!

Hermia: Oh, I had a horrible dream that you were gone, Lysander. Lysander? Where have you gone? Oh, no! Where is my love? I must find him!

Act III, Scene I

In another part of the woods

Oberon: Ah Puck, what news have you for me?

Puck: Titania is in love with a man who has a donkey head! It is a humorous sight to see.

Oberon: And how did you make this happen, clever Puck?

Puck: There was a troop of terrible actors rehearsing their play beneath the glen where Titania slept. After I changed the worst of the actors into a half-donkey, half-man, his crazed noises woke Titania. It was done; the flower's pollen worked and now she loves this hideous and ridiculous creature!

Oberon: This worked better than I had planned! But, Puck, did you find the young man and woman and ensure his love for her?

Puck: That is done, as well. Look, here they come now.

Hermia: What have you done to my Lysander? Have you harmed him? I will never forgive you if you have.

Demetrius: Do not be angry with me, Hermia. I did not hurt Lysander in any way, even though I would like to.

Hermia: Then where is he?

Demetrius: What will you give me if I tell you?

Hermia: The gift of never having to see me, since I have no desire to see you again as long as I live.

Demetrius: There is no reasoning with you when you are in this particular mood. I am tired and will lie down here for a short rest.

Oberon: Puck, you foolish sprite! Now you have taken two lovers and separated them instead of making two others fall in love. Go quickly and find a young woman named Helena. She is in love with this man lying here. Bring her here, and I will place the pollen on his eyes so when he awakens, he will be in love with her, too.

Puck: Do not worry, I will go and find her straightaway.

Oberon: Pollen of this pink flower: work on this man your magic power. When Helena comes wandering near, awake Demetrius and hold her dear.

Puck:	King Oberon, Helena is coming, and she is being followed by the young man on whom I placed the pollen. He is madly in love with her and pleads for her attention. Shall we watch how this all plays out? Lord, what fools these mortals be!
Oberon:	Let us stand over here and watch. The noise they are making will surely awaken Demetrius.
Lysander:	Why do you think that when I vow my love, I am mocking you, beautiful Helena?
Helena:	Lysander, this is beyond cruel. Please stop. I know that you love Hermia, and I know this is some kind of joke for the two of you, but stop! As you know very well, I love only Demetrius.
Lysander:	But Demetrius loves Hermia, not you. Let him have her, and I will have you. Look, he is right here and is waking up now.
Demetrius:	Goddess, perfect, divine, Helena. My darling!
Helena:	No! This joke has gone too far. I see that you are all in on it. I understand that you want to hurt my feelings, Demetrius, but this is completely unfair. This change of heart is too cruel, for you have all joined against me to make me look foolish.

Lysander: Yes, Demetrius, you are far too callous and mean for my dear Helena. You love Hermia, and I freely give Hermia to you, as I no longer care for her. I will take care of my real love, my Helena.

Demetrius: No! No, Lysander! You were right. You should keep Hermia. I was foolish not to see the perfection that is Helena. Here comes Hermia now. We must tell her.

Hermia: Oh, Lysander. I have been looking for you all over these woods! Why did you leave me alone?

Lysander: I had no reason to stay with you.

Hermia: What do you mean?

Lysander: When Helena came by, I saw my folly in loving you and knew I must follow her.

Hermia: This cannot be true.

Helena: You are part of this, too? I knew that men could be cruel to women and their soft souls. But you, Hermia? We have been friends since childhood.

Hermia: I do not know what you mean.

Helena:	You know both men adore you. Did you not ask Lysander to pursue me with words of love as a way to pierce my heart? And then, you bade Demetrius to do the same. It is a mean-spirited joke and is beneath you!
Hermia:	I know nothing about it, Helena.
Helena:	Fine, continue this joke, Hermia, but never ask me to be your friend again. I am leaving!
Lysander:	No, sweet Helena, do not leave!
Hermia:	Stop, Lysander! Whatever this is, stop it! You can see that you are greatly upsetting Helena.
Lysander:	Stop, Helena! I love you!
Demetrius:	I love you more, Helena!
Lysander:	Draw your sword and prove it, you scoundrel!
Demetrius:	Gladly, you fool!
Hermia:	Lysander, what are you doing? Stop!

Lysander:	Unhand me, Hermia, you ugly little thing.
Hermia:	What are you saying, Lysander?
Demetrius:	Come and fight, Lysander! You snake!
Lysander:	Get off me, Hermia! Go away, you vile thing!
Hermia:	Are you joking, Lysander?
Helena:	Yes, and so are you.
Demetrius:	Lysander, are you too big a coward to fight?
Lysander:	I will fight you, but Hermia is in my way. What do you want me to do with her? Although I never want to lay eyes on her again, I will not hurt her.
Hermia:	But you are hurting me with your words! Am I not Hermia, and you, Lysander? Just a few short hours ago, you loved me and wanted to be with me forever. We were to be married.
Lysander:	Married! Ha! You disgust me. I love Helena.
Hermia:	Helena, this is all your fault!

Helena: My fault! This is *your* joke, *your* puppet show.

Hermia: A puppet? Now you are making fun of my being short! Is that what you did? You came with your tall and lanky body and stole Lysander's love. Do you think that I cannot reach you? Well, I am not that short. I can reach your eyes with my nails.

Helena: Please, good gentlemen, although you all mock me, do not let Hermia hurt me. Perhaps because she is so little you might think she will not—

Hermia: "Little" again! Stop making fun of my height!

Helena: Hermia, I was always a good friend to you. I did you no wrong, except once, and that was to tell Demetrius that you were running away into the woods. But my intention was to follow him and win him over. I will leave now.

Hermia: Fine, go then! What is keeping you?

Helena: A love that is hard to let go of.

Hermia: For Lysander?

Helena: No, for Demetrius.

Lysander:	Do not fear, Helena, this dwarf cannot harm you.
Demetrius:	No, I will protect you, Helena.
Lysander:	We will fight farther off in the woods for the love and honor of Helena.
Helena:	I do not trust you, Hermia. I am leaving.
Hermia:	I am heartsick and speechless. I am leaving, too.
Oberon:	This is entirely your fault, Puck.
Puck:	All you told me was to find a young man and a young woman. You can see how I could have been mistaken, but you must admit that they are entertaining to watch!
Oberon:	We must fix this. Lysander and Demetrius seek a place to fight, so I want you to interrupt their search by making it foggy. Do not allow them to find each other. Disguise your voice to sound like them, calling to each other so that they get lost and cannot fight. Make sure that you bring all four of them together, close enough to know one another when they awaken but far enough apart so there will be no more chaos tonight.

Puck: I will do exactly as you say, King Oberon.

Oberon: Once they are asleep, place this potion into Lysander's eyes to remove the pollen you mistakenly placed. Then his love will swiftly return to Hermia. They will think of tonight's actions as a dream. I will now get my servant boy from Titania and release her from her love spell. Meet me there when you are finished.

Puck: Yes, King Oberon. The couples will be together in the morning, and I will see you soon.

Act IV, Scene I

In the woods near Titania

Oberon: Puck, I hope you did just as I told you.

Puck: I did, King Oberon. What is happening here?

Oberon: Titania was busy fawning over that fool, Bottom, and I felt sorry for her. However, I was able to get the boy without a fuss. Now, I will remove this charm from her eyes. Puck, you must end your prank, as well. Take the donkey spell off this man, and just like you did with the couples, have him remember this night as only a dream.

Puck: Do not worry, for I will do exactly what you wish.

Oberon: Now for my part, Titania. Be as you used to be; see as you used to see; from your love for this beast, with this flower you are released.

Puck: I see the morning sun just peeking over the horizon. With everything the way it should be now, we must prepare for the wedding celebration of Theseus and Hippolyta.

Act IV, Scene II

In the woods

Hermia: Last night was so strange for all of us, but this morning was even stranger and more wonderful.

Lysander: Yes, having your father, Theseus, and Hippolyta find all of us in the woods turned out wonderfully.

Demetrius: What strange dreams we had! But once they saw that Helena and I love each other, and you two love each other, they suggested we all get married at tonight's ceremony. I could not be happier.

Helena: Neither could I, dear Demetrius. Now, we must all ready ourselves for our weddings this evening.

Act IV, Scene III

At the wedding ceremonies

Demetrius: Now that we are all happily married, I cannot wait to sit down and enjoy the entertainment. I heard some local men will be performing a play for us this evening.

Helena: It should be a wonderful way to end the celebration. But, I have been warned that these men may not be too intelligent.

Lysander: But we cannot level any judgment against them if they are performing with good hearts and good intent.

Hermia: Listen, the first actor has spoken the whole prologue without taking a breath. He must be nervous.

Lysander: It is funny how they explain who plays a wall and who plays a lion. They fumble so with their parts.

Demetrius: I am amused that they tell us each time they come and leave, and what is real and what is not, as if we cannot tell by watching it. It is a love story, but quite silly.

Helena:	I think it is finally over. They want us to cheer.
Lysander:	Yes, you are right. Actors, thank you for your play. It is almost midnight, and it is time for bed. I hope for sweet dreams tonight and always.
Oberon:	Puck, I know the happy couples cannot see or hear us, but I have a wedding gift for them. From now until the sun rises, I asked the fairies to go through this house and bless each couple so that their lives are rich with love. Now, Puck, meet me in the woods before the sun rises.
Puck:	Good people of the audience, if this play has offended you, think of it this way: it was no more than a dream. So good night, dear friends, and applaud as our play comes to an end.

Song: Sonnet 154

Sonnet 57

William Shakespeare

Being your slave, what should I do but tend
Upon the hours and times of your desire?
I have no precious time at all to spend,
Nor services to do, till you require.
Nor dare I chide the world-without-end hour,
Whilst I, my sovereign, watch the clock for you,
Nor think the bitterness of absence sour,
When you have bid your servant once adieu
Nor dare I question with my jealous thought
Where you may be, or your affairs suppose,
But like a sad slave stay and think of nought
Save where you are how happy you make those.
    So true a fool is love that in your will,
    Though you do any thing he thinks no ill.

Sonnet 154

 ## William Shakespeare

The little Love-god lying once asleep
Laid by his side his heart-inflaming brand,
Whilst many nymphs that vow'd chaste life to keep
Came tripping by, but in her maiden hand
The fairest votary took up that fire,
Which many legions of true hearts had warm'd;
And so the general of hot desire
Was sleeping by a virgin hand disarm'd.
This brand she quenched in a cool well by,
Which from Love's fire took heat perpetual,
Growing a bath and healthful remedy
For men diseased, but I, my mistress' thrall,
  Came there for cure, and this by that I prove:
  Love's fire heats water, water cools not love.

Glossary

acquiesce—to accept, agree, or give consent by keeping silent or by not raising objections

bade—command

callous—feeling or showing no sympathy for others

chaste—pure in thought and act

chide—to express a mild disapproval of

Cupid—god of love in Roman mythology

downtrodden—crushed by superior power

glen—a narrow, hidden valley

headstrong—not easily controlled; wanting one's own way

henchman—a trusted follower or supporter

lark—any of numerous Old World singing birds that are usually brownish in color and live on the ground

nymphs—several of many goddesses in old legends represented as beautiful young girls living in mountains, forests, meadows, and waters

perpetual—occurring continually

sovereign—a person in supreme power or authority

sprite—a fairy

votary—a devoted follower